Tell Me A Story

by Susan Grant

illustrated by Christopher M. Dall

Produced by:

FriesenPress
Suite 300 – 852 Fort Street
Victoria, BC, Canada V8W 1H8

www.friesenpress.com

Distributed to the trade by The Ingram Book Company

Thank you, Mom,
for being the best storyteller of all time.

For Ella, Nicholas and Aiden,
with love.

Dippy Ducky

Once upon a time there were two duckies. A mommy and a little baby named Dippy Ducky. They loved each other soooooooooooo much.

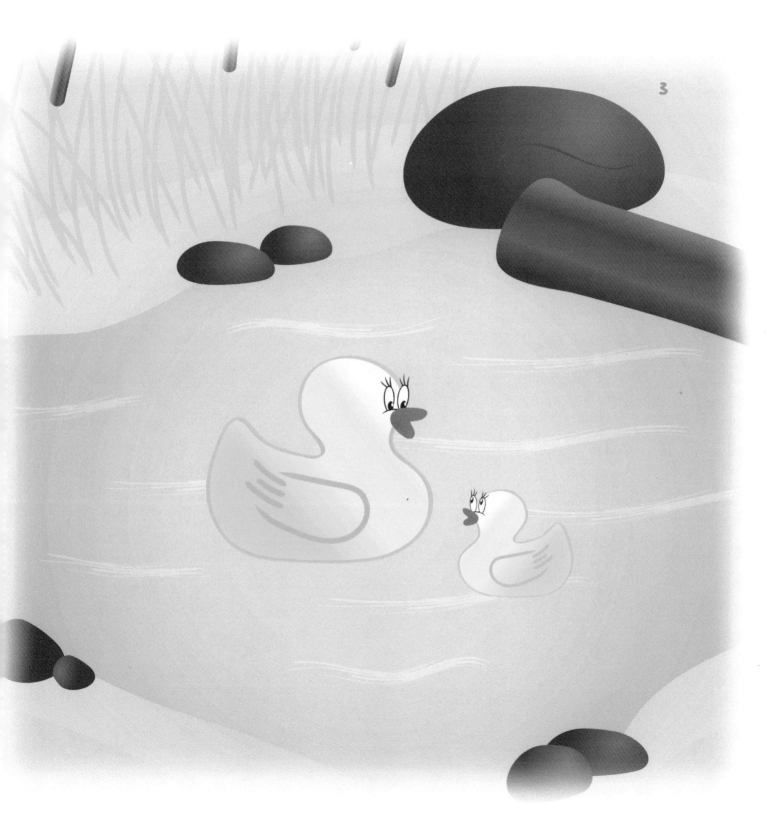

One day, Dippy Ducky and Mommy Ducky were swimming in the pond. Mommy Ducky showed Dippy Ducky a big rock and said, "See that rock over there?"

"Yes, Mommy, I see the rock."

"You must promise Mommy that you will never go to that rock. It is very dangerous there, because that is where Sammy Snake lives, and he is not a very nice snake."

"Ok Mommy, I won't go there." said Dippy Ducky.

The next day, Dippy Ducky was swimming around while Mommy Ducky was making lunch. Dippy Ducky saw that there was a lot of candy on the rock and the candy looked so delicious.

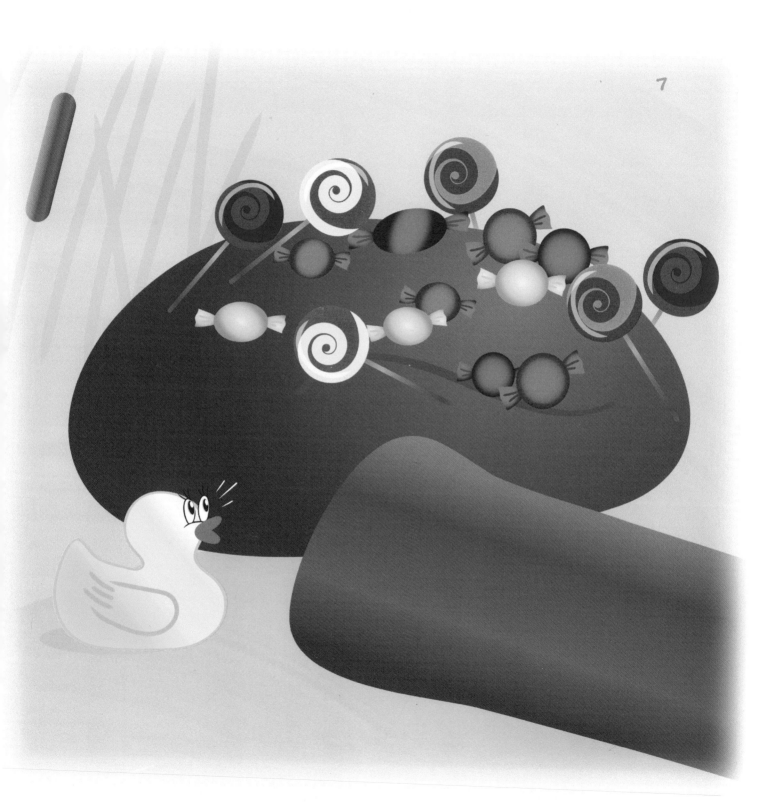

Dippy Ducky knew that his mommy had told him not to go to the rock, but he really wanted the candy and his mommy was busy. He thought maybe he could go get the candy and come back before his mommy knew he had gone. So, he swam to the rock and started to eat the candy.

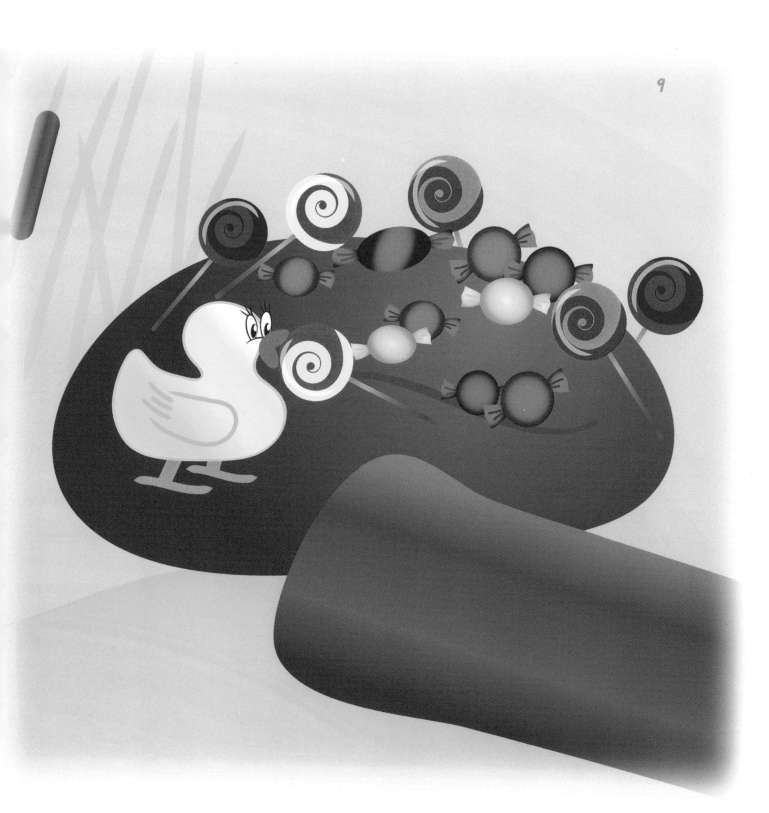

Suddenly, he heard a big sound.

"BOO!" Sammy Snake scared Dippy Ducky and said he was going to catch him.

Dippy Ducky was very scared. He started to cry and tried to swim home as fast as he could. He hoped that Sammy Snake could not catch him.

"Where were you Dippy? I was so worried about you! Are you okay?" Mommy Ducky hugged Dippy Ducky.

"Yes, Mommy. I am okay. I am sorry. I went to the rock to eat candy and the snake scared me and wanted to catch me." Dippy Ducky was still crying.

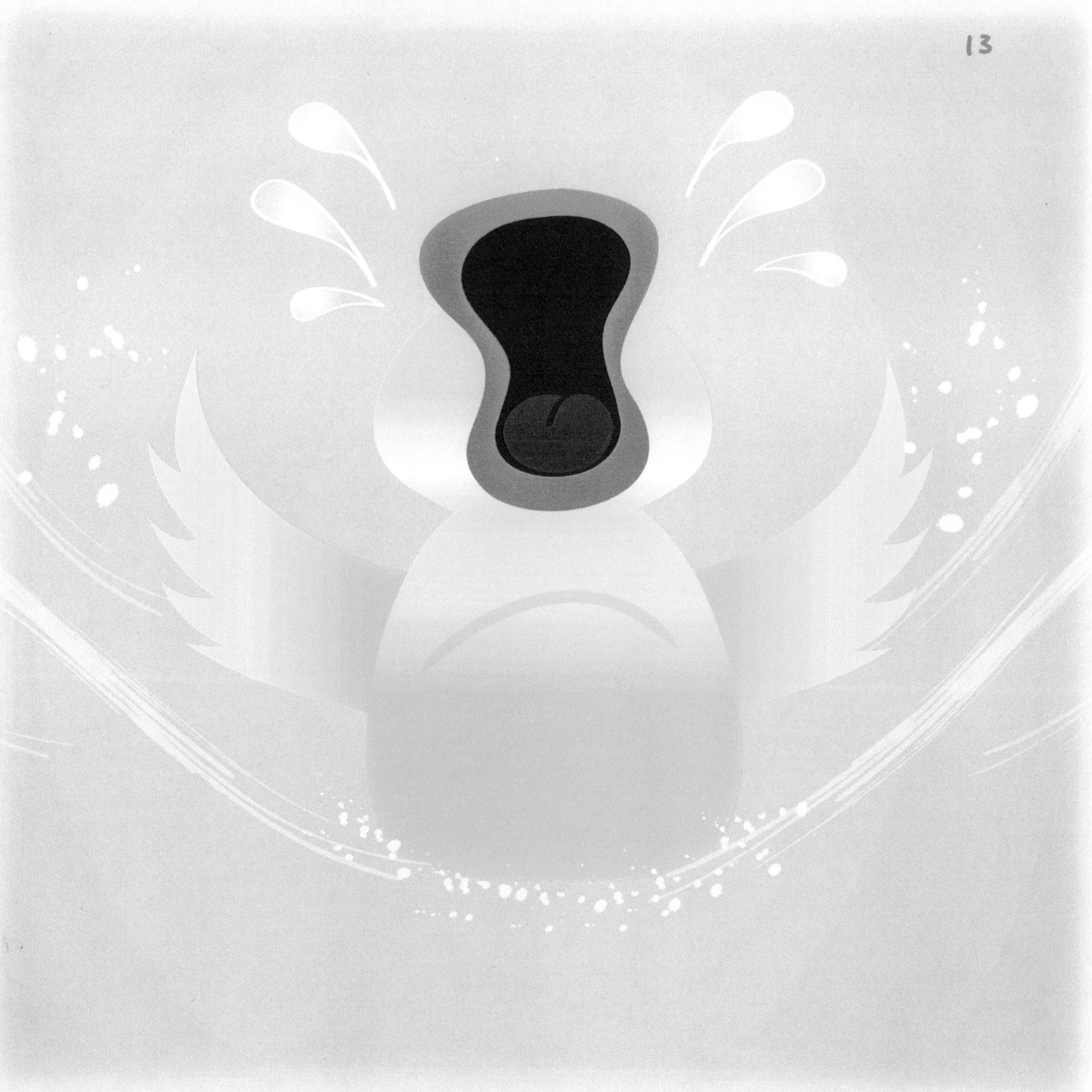

"Well, I am glad you are ok. I love you so much my sweet little Dippy Ducky. I am glad you are okay. I hope you learned your lesson." said Mommy Ducky as she wiped his tears.

"Yes I did. I am sorry, Mommy."

"Remember, Sweetheart, you always have to listen to your Mommy."

Dippy Ducky and Mommy Ducky hugged each other and Dippy Ducky promised that he would always listen to his mommy.

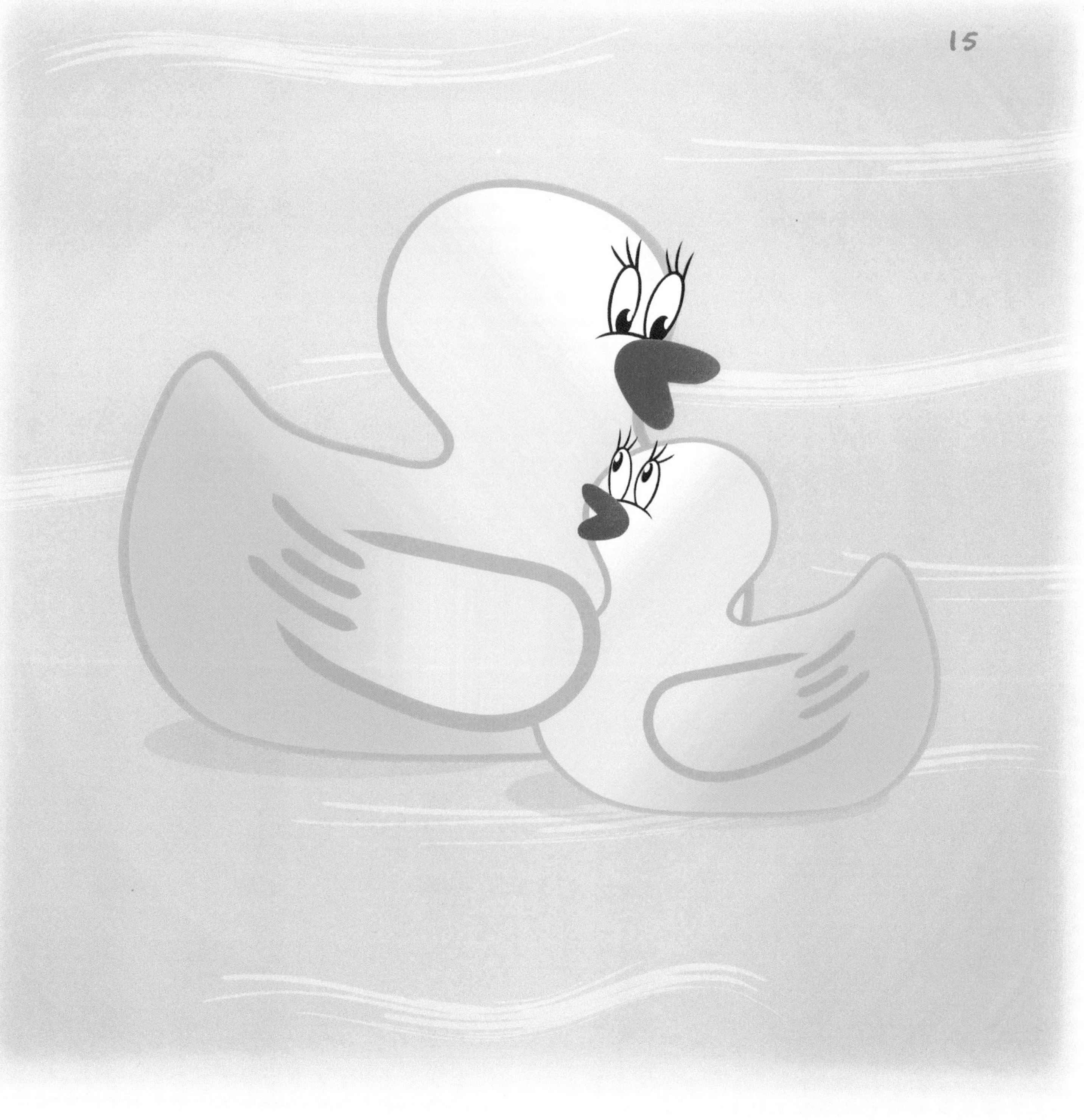

Playing in the Park

Once upon a time there was a little girl named Mary and a little boy named Nicholas. Mary and Nicholas were in the park. Nicholas wanted very much to play with Mary, but Mary did not want to play with Nicholas.

When Nicholas wanted to share Mary's toys, Mary would say, "NO!"

When Nicholas wanted to go down the slide with Mary, she told him to go away.

When Nicholas wanted to play on the swings with Mary, she told him she didn't want to play with him.

Nicholas became very sad that Mary wouldn't play with him. He sat down in the sand and started to cry.

Then, a little girl named Ella came skipping along and saw that little Nicholas was sitting on the sand looking very sad. She went over to see him.

"What's your name?" she asked.

"My name is Nicholas," the little boy said quietly.

"Why are you sad, Nicholas?"

"Because Mary is not being nice to me and I want to play with her."

"That's okay, Nicholas, I will play with you," said Ella

Ella and Nicholas started to play together and had so much fun. They were running in the sand, jumping on the grass, swinging on the swings and racing down the slide. Nicholas was not upset anymore.

Ella then decided to go and talk to Mary. She told Mary that she should always be nice to other kids, and that she must remember to share. Mary said that she was sorry and asked if she could come and play with Ella and Nicholas.

Ella, Nicholas and Mary all started to play together and have fun. Mary promised that from now on she would always be a very nice girl.

32

Peter and the Bird

Once upon a time there was a little boy named Peter. It was cold and snowing outside while Peter was sitting by his window reading a book. Suddenly, Peter heard tapping at his window. He put down his book to see what was making that noise.

Peter saw that it was a little baby bird. The baby bird looked very sad, tired and cold. Peter quickly opened the window and brought the baby bird inside. He wrapped a small blanket around the baby bird to keep him nice and warm. He decided to name him JooJoo.

JooJoo was getting warmer but seemed thirsty. So, Peter went downstairs to see his mommy.

"Mommy, can I please have some warm water?"

"Why do you need warm water?"

"Because I found a little cold baby bird and he needs some."

"Okay, Peter, let me get some for you."

So Peter took the warm water and gave it to the JooJoo. He slowly drank it and started to feel better.

The next day, Peter's daddy came home with a cage to put Peter's baby bird in. Peter was so happy. He put JooJoo in the cage beside his window. Peter loved having him in his room.

JooJoo loved Peter, but would always look at his friends playing outside.

One day, Peter's daddy came to Peter's room to talk to him.

"Peter, I think it would be a good idea for you to let JooJoo out of the cage and fly outside with all the other birdies, because that is where all his friends are and his mommy and daddy are. It was very nice of you to take care of him when he wasn't well, but I think he is better now."

Peter agreed with his daddy that it was time to let JooJoo go outside again.

Peter opened the cage, held little JooJoo in his hand and opened the window. He gave him a little kiss on the head and told him to fly away. JooJoo gave Peter a kiss and turned and flew away to his friends and his family.

From then on the JooJoo would always happily play with his friends outside, but he would always come back to Peter's window to visit him.

CPSIA information can be obtained
at www.ICGtesting.com
Printed in the USA
LVIC04n0303110913
351849LV00001B

9 781460 213568